Mr. Putter & Tabby
Toot the Horn

CYNTHIA RYLANT

Mr. Putter & Tabby
Toot the Horn

Illustrated by

ARTHUR HOWARD

Harcourt Brace & Company

San Diego   New York   London

For my son, Nate, who's always appreciated loud music
—C. R.

For Allyn and Susan
—A. H.

Text copyright © 1998 by Cynthia Rylant
Illustrations copyright © 1998 by Arthur Howard

Requests for permission to make
copies of any part of the work should be mailed to:
Permissions Department, Harcourt Brace & Company,
6277 Sea Harbor Drive,
Orlando, Florida 32887-6777.

Library of Congress Cataloging-in-Publication Data
Rylant, Cynthia.
Mr. Putter & Tabby toot the horn/Cynthia Rylant;
illustrated by Arthur Howard.
p.   cm.
Summary: Mr. Putter's neighbor, Mrs. Teaberry, decides
that they should join a band, but finding the right one
isn't as easy as it sounds—for them or their pets.
ISBN 0-15-200244-8
[1. Old age—Fiction. 2. Neighbors—Fiction. 3. Music—Fiction.]
I. Howard, Arthur, ill. II. Title.
PZ7.R982Muf   1998
[Fic]—dc20   96-41768

Printed in Singapore

First edition
A C E F D B

1

Loud Music

2

Tough Teeth

3

Mr. Putter Can't

4

Mr. Putter Tries

5

The Band

1

Loud Music

Mr. Putter and his fine cat, Tabby,
were neighbors to Mrs. Teaberry
and her good dog, Zeke.
Mrs. Teaberry and Mr. Putter
had a lot in common.

They both liked bingo.

They both liked free samples.

They both liked rain.

And they both liked music.
Mrs. Teaberry liked country music
the best.
She liked the broken hearts.
She liked the big silver boots
and the tall hair.

Mr. Putter liked opera.

He also liked broken hearts.

And he liked the big round heroes

and the violins.

Some days Mrs. Teaberry would play
her country music very loud
for Mr. Putter to hear.
Some days Mr. Putter would play
his opera very loud
for Mrs. Teaberry to hear.
They liked sharing.

One day Mrs. Teaberry
had an idea.
"We should join a band,"
she told Mr. Putter.

"But I can't join a band," said Mr. Putter.

"I can't play an instrument."

"Of course you can," said Mrs. Teaberry.

"Old people can do anything they want."

"Can they say they can't play an
instrument?" asked Mr. Putter.
"No," said Mrs. Teaberry.
So she and Mr. Putter went to look
for a band.

2

Tough Teeth

Mr. Putter and Tabby
and Mrs. Teaberry and Zeke
went to hear many bands play.
They went to hear an Irish band play jigs.

But the jigging made Tabby nervous
and Zeke itch.
So they could not play in
an Irish band.

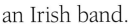

Next they went to hear a brass band.
But the brassy sound made
Mrs. Teaberry's teeth hurt.
So they could not play in a brass band.

Then they went to hear a jazz band.
The band played very late, in a club,
after midnight.
Mr. Putter fell asleep.
So they could not play in a jazz band.

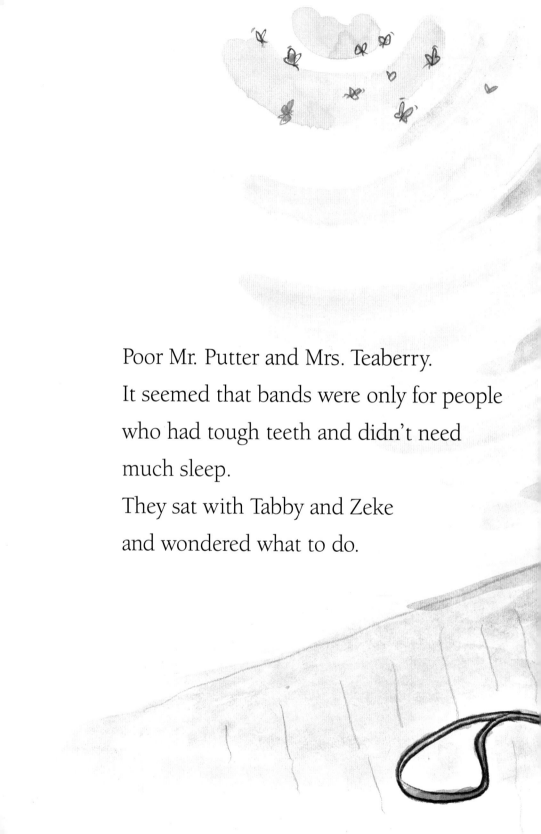

Poor Mr. Putter and Mrs. Teaberry.
It seemed that bands were only for people
who had tough teeth and didn't need
much sleep.
They sat with Tabby and Zeke
and wondered what to do.

3

Mr. Putter Can't

"I have it!" said Mrs. Teaberry
a few days later.
She had brought Mr. Putter and Tabby
some peach tea and a carrot pie.
"*We* will be a band!"

"But I still can't play an instrument,"
said Mr. Putter.
"Of course you can,"
said Mrs. Teaberry.
"I can't," said Mr. Putter.
"You can if you want to,"
said Mrs. Teaberry.

Mr. Putter thought about
Tabby's nerves

and Zeke's itch

and Mrs. Teaberry's teeth.

He thought about a nap.
"I'm not sure if I want to,"
said Mr. Putter.

"If you try, I will bake you
something sweet,"
said Mrs. Teaberry.
"Sweet?" said Mr. Putter.

"Something really nutty,"
said Mrs. Teaberry.
"Nutty?" said Mr. Putter.
"With lots of vanilla," said Mrs. Teaberry.
"I'm ready to play!" said Mr. Putter.

4

Mr. Putter Tries

The next day Mr. Putter
bought a little horn.
He bought it because it was on sale.

When he got home,
Mr. Putter tooted
the horn for four hours.

He was a very
bad tooter.
The worst.

Tabby went outside to sleep
in the ferns.

Mrs. Teaberry did not buy
a horn to toot.
She bought a mandolin.
When she got home,
she started plucking.
She was a *good* plucker.
She plucked all night long,
and Zeke did not itch.

By the next morning, Mrs. Teaberry
could pluck her favorite country songs.

But Mr. Putter could not toot
his favorite songs.
His tooter was holding up a tomato plant.

5

The Band

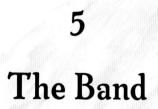

Mrs. Teaberry forgave Mr. Putter
for being a bad tooter.
She said he could listen to her
pluck instead.
So he did.

He listened to her pluck
all the brokenhearted songs
she could think of.
He liked it very much.
Tabby purred.
Zeke did not itch.

After the concert they all
had a sweet, nutty, vanilla surprise.

Mrs. Teaberry said Mr. Putter deserved it
because he had tried.

She said she did not mind being
the only person in the band.
She said the name of her band would be
"Plucking Without Putter."
And they laughed and laughed
and laughed.

The illustrations in this book were done in pencil, watercolor,
gouache, and Sennelier pastels on 90-pound vellum paper.
The display type was set in Artcraft and
the text type was set in Berkeley Old Style Book.
Color separations by Bright Arts, Ltd., Singapore
Printed and bound by Tien Wah Press, Singapore
This book was printed on totally chlorine-free
Nymolla Matte Art paper.
Production supervision by Stanley Redfern
Designed by Arthur Howard and Carolyn Stafford